3

And then
shattering
into
millions of
drops

Now that I think of it, the story was probably painful for her.

All those **memories** of a world **lost forever.**

But she told it with a **gentle smile,** helping me to fall comfortably asleep.

Sometimes, she changed the story a little, just to see how I would react.

Before I tell you **my story**, I'll recount nan's night-time tale.

Because that's where it all began.

Even though it took me **a long time** to realise that.

I'm sorry about any historical inconsistencies that you may find.

After all, this is a **memory** of a memory!

5

London, 2063

The world was
very different from
what it is today.

Mostly because,
despite evidence of
a dying planet, people
still held on to

hope.

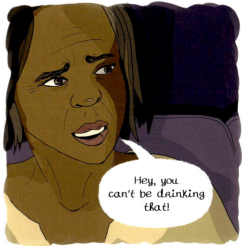

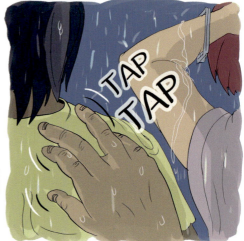

My grandmother told me that the man looked **quite sad,** so she gave him a big **warm hug.**

(she was never the spontaneous type, but I guess she must have been **caught up in the moment.**)

Nan never told me what
a mortgage was, or why the
stranger thought that she
should know about his.

But perhaps she didn't
want to dwell on it...

... because there was a turn
of events right afterwards.

This is the story of how my family
experienced their last day of rain...

... and also of how I was born.

(I was a rather ugly baby)

As for the man, well...

He vanished with the rain.

2091

London, **2091**

28 years had gone by since **the last day of rain** in the city.

The **scorching heat** dried up the atmosphere, so clouds didn't stand a chance of forming.

I dreamt of seeing water coming from the sky.

To feel it. To smell it.

To be one with the raindrops and join their fortuitous symphony.

But maybe it was an impossible dream.

And I had made a few **bad decisions** while pursuing it.

To be continued!

Follow me on social media or
subscribe to the newsletter to find out
when the next chapters are available!

thelastdayofrain.com
claudiamatosa.com
@claudiamatosa